Waiting for the Biblioburro

by Monica Brown

Illustrations by John Parra

TRICYCLE PRESS

Berkeley

Acknowledgments

The author would like to acknowledge Simon Romero of the *New York Times* and Valentina Canavesio of Ayoka Productions, who shed light on Luis Soriano Bohórquez's work for literacy. Most special thanks, however, go to Luis himself, for his participation and support of this book.

Text copyright © 2011 by Monica Brown
Illustrations copyright © 2011 by John Parra

Library of Congress Cataloging-in-Publication Data
Brown, Monica, 1969–
Waiting for the Biblioburro / by Monica Brown ; illustrations by John Parra. — 1st ed.
p. cm.
Summary: When a man brings to a remote village two burros, Alfa and Beto, loaded with books the children can borrow, Ana's excitement leads her to write a book of her own as she waits for the Biblioburro to return. Includes glossary of Spanish terms and a note on the true story of Colombia's Biblioburro and mobile libraries in other countries.
[1. Biblioburro—Fiction. 2. Books and reading—Fiction. 3. Libraries—Fiction. 4. Soriano, Luis—Fiction. 5. Colombia—Fiction.] I. Parra, John, ill. II. Title.
PZ7.B816644Wai 2011
[E]—dc22
2010024183
ISBN 978-1-58246-353-7 (hardcover) • ISBN 978-1-58246-398-8 (Gibraltar lib. bdg.)

Printed in Malaysia

Design by Chloe Rawlins
Typeset in Celestia Antiqua and Putain
The illustrations are acrylics on board.

13 14 15 16 17 18 19 20 – 16 15 14

First Edition

For Luis Soriano Bohórquez, Nicole Geiger, and
all who put books into the hands of children.
—M.B.

For Jacob, Elizabeth, and Allison Parra:
may your imaginations be your guide in life.
—J.P.

BURRO

On a hill behind a tree, there is a house.
In the house, there is a bed and on the bed
there is a little girl named Ana, fast asleep,
dreaming about the world outside and
beyond the hill.

When Ana wakes up to the rooster's *quiquiriquí*,
Papi is already at work on the farm and Mami is busy
in the garden. Ana bathes her little brother and feeds
the goats and collects the eggs to sell at the market.

After breakfast, Ana and her mother walk down the hill. Ana closes her eyes against the sun and wishes she was back in the cool of the house with her *libro*, her book.

Ana has read her book, her only book, so many times she knows it by heart. The book was a gift from her teacher for working so hard on her reading and writing. But last fall, her teacher moved far away, and now there is no one to teach Ana and the other children in her village.

So, at night, on her bed in the house on the hill, Ana makes up her own *cuentos* and tells the stories to her little brother to help him fall asleep. She tells him stories about make-believe creatures that live in the forest and the mountains and the sea. She wishes for new stories to read, but her teacher with the books has gone.

One morning, Ana wakes up to the sounds of *tacatac!*
Clip-clop! and a loud *iii-aah, iii-aah!*

When Ana looks down the hill below her house she sees
a man with a sign that reads B*iblioburro*. With the man,
there are two *burros*. What are they carrying?

Libros! Books!

Ana runs down the hill to the man with the sign and the *burros* and the books. Other children run to him too, skipping down hills and stomping through the fields.

"Who are you? Who are they?" the children ask.

The man says, "I am a librarian, a *bibliotecario*, and these are my *burros*, Alfa and Beto. Welcome to the Biblioburro, my *biblioteca*."

"But, *señor*," Ana says, "I thought libraries were only in big cities and buildings."

"Not this one," says the librarian. "This is a *moving* library."

Then he spreads out his books and invites the children to join him under a tree.

"Once upon a time," the librarian begins, sharing the story of an elephant who swings from a spider's web. He reads from books with beautiful pictures, then helps the little ones learn their *abecedario*.

He sings, "A, B, C, D, E, F, G . . ."

Finally, he says, "Now it's your turn. Pick out books and in a few weeks I will be back to collect them and bring you new ones."

"Me too?" asks Ana.

"Especially you," says the librarian with a smile.

So many *cuentos*!

While Alfa and Beto chomp the sweet grass under the tree, Ana picks up book after book and finds pink dolphins and blue butterflies, castles and fairies, talking lions and magic carpets.

"Someone should write a story about your *burros*,"
Ana tells the librarian, rubbing Alfa's nose and feeding
more grass to Beto.

"Why don't you?" he asks. Then he packs up the books,
and is off.

"Enjoy!" he calls to the children. "I will be back."

Ana runs up the hill to her house, hugging the books
to her chest. She can't wait to share her books with
her brother, and that night she reads until she can't
keep her eyes open any longer.

domingo
21ST

6TH

sábado

viernes

17TH

"When will he come back?" she asks her mother,
who smiles and says, "Go read, Ana."

"When will he come back?" she asks her mother,
who smiles and says, "Go draw, Ana."

"When will he come back?" she asks her mother,
who smiles and says, "Go write, Ana."

"When will he come back?" she asks her mother,
who finally says, "Go to bed, Ana!"

Each morning Ana does her chores and reads and looks
out her window. She listens for the sounds of Alfa and
Beto, but weeks pass, and the librarian doesn't return.

One night, Ana dreams she is flying over her country on a butterfly's back. In her dream she crosses mountains and oceans and rivers and jungles, bringing stories everywhere she goes. Stories fly from her mouth and fingers like magic, falling into the hands of the children waiting below.

When Ana wakes up she misses Alfa and Beto and the Biblioburro's books. She remembers that the librarian told her that she could write a book, and so, with paper and string and colored pencils, she does.

Finally, just when Ana thinks she'll never see the Biblioburro again, she wakes up to *iii-aah, iii-aah!* and children yelling.

She runs down the hill with her library books and a special surprise of her very own.

"I wrote this *cuento* for you," she says.

"*¡Qué bueno!*" the librarian says and then he reads *her* story to the children under the tree.

When it's time to go, Ana's book is packed carefully
on the *burro*'s back, ready to be carried away, over the
hills and through the fields to another child who is . . .

asleep on a bed, in a house, on a hill behind a tree,
dreaming of Alfa and Beto and all the new stories
the Biblioburro will bring.

AUTHOR'S NOTE

How far would you go for a book? How far would a librarian travel to bring a book to you?

Around the world, there are many librarians, and libraries, that travel long distances, just like the Biblioburro. In Kenya, camel caravans deliver books to nomads in the desert. In Sweden, Stockholm's "floating library" delivers books to islanders on book boats. In Zimbabwe, there is a donkey-drawn mobile cart library. In the United States, bookmobiles started out as book wagons.

This book was inspired by a particular librarian I was honored to get to know—Luis Soriano Bohórquez. Near La Gloria, Colombia, this teacher and librarian delivers books to children who live in remote villages with the help of his two donkeys, Alfa and Beto. Luis's Biblioburro program is an inspiration to us all. To learn more about Luis, check out www.cnn.com/2010/LIVING/02/25/cnnheroes.soriano/.

This book is a celebration of Luis and all the teachers and librarians who bring books to children everywhere—across deserts, fields, mountains and water.

GLOSSARY OF SPANISH TERMS

abecedario: alphabet

biblioteca: library

bibliotecario: librarian

burro: donkey

cuento: story

domingo: Sunday

había una vez: once upon a time

iii-aah: hee-haw

jueves: Thursday

libro: book

lunes: Monday

martes: Tuesday

miércoles: Wednesday

qué bueno: that's good

quiquiriquí: cock-a-doodle-doo

sábado: Saturday

señor: sir

tacatac: clip-clop

viernes: Friday